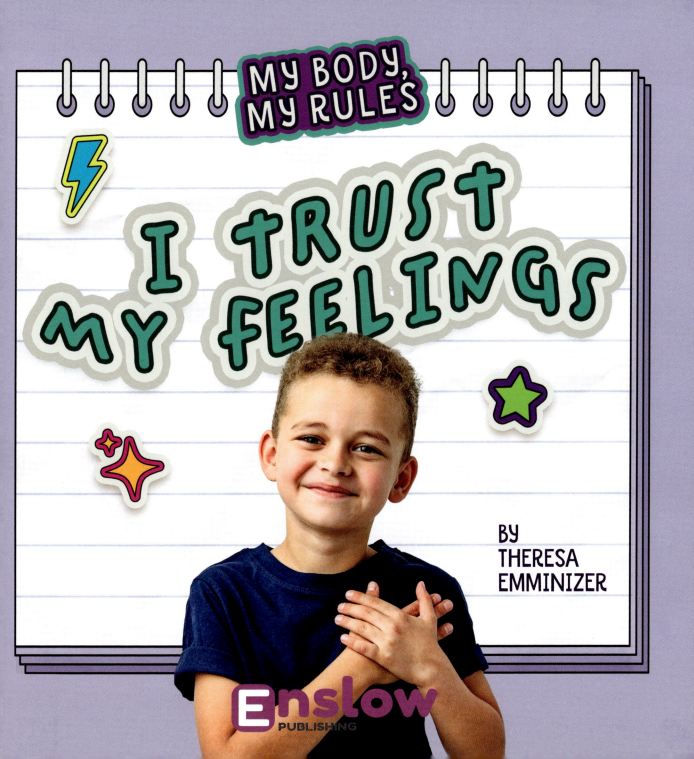

MY BODY, MY RULES

I TRUST MY FEELINGS

BY THERESA EMMINIZER

Enslow PUBLISHING

Please visit our website, www.enslow.com.
For a free color catalog of all our high-quality books, call toll free
1-800-398-2504 or fax 1-877-980-4454.

Library of Congress Cataloging-in-Publication Data

Names: Emminizer, Theresa, author.
Title: I trust my feelings / Theresa Emminizer.
Description: Buffalo : Enslow Publishing, [2025] | Series: My body, my
  rules | Includes index. | Audience: Grades K-1
Identifiers: LCCN 2023053906 (print) | LCCN 2023053907 (ebook) | ISBN
  9781978539419 (library binding) | ISBN 9781978539402 (paperback) | ISBN
  9781978539426 (ebook)
Subjects: LCSH: Emotions–Juvenile literature. | Emotions in
  children–Juvenile literature,
Classification: LCC BF723.E6 .E66 2025 (print) | LCC BF723.E6 (ebook) |
  DDC 155.4/124–dc23/eng/20231218
LC record available at https://lccn.loc.gov/2023053906
LC ebook record available at https://lccn.loc.gov/2023053907

Published in 2025 by
Enslow Publishing
2544 Clinton Street
Buffalo, NY 14224

Copyright © 2025 Enslow Publishing

Designer: Tanya Dellaccio Keeney
Editor: Theresa Emminizer

Photo credits: Series art (notebook) Design PRESENT/Shutterstock.com; series art (stickers) tmn art/Shutterstock.com; cover (boy) UfaBizPhoto/Shutterstock.com; p. 5 Africa Studio/Shutterstock.com; p. 7 (top left) Asier Romero/Shutterstock.com; p. 7 (top right, bottom left) Prostock-studio/Shutterstock.com; p. 7 (bottom right) TimeImage Production/Shutterstock.com; p. 9 krakenimages.com/Shutterstock.com; p. 11 Prostock-studio/Shutterstock.com; pp. 13, 15, 19 fizkes/Shutterstock.com; p. 17 VGstockstudio/Shutterstock.com; p. 21 Studio Romantic/Shutterstock.com.

All rights reserved.
No part of this book may be reproduced in any form without permission in writing from the publisher, except by a reviewer.

Printed in the United States of America

Some of the images in this book illustrate individuals who are models. The depictions do not imply actual situations or events.

CPSIA compliance information: Batch #CSENS25: For further information contact Enslow Publishing, at 1-800-398-2504.

CONTENTS

LISTEN IN 4
NAME THAT FEELING 6
THE "UH-OH" FEELING 8
FEELINGS ARE FRIENDS 10
SHARE YOUR FEELINGS 12
MAKE A SAFETY CIRCLE 14
FEELING CONFUSED 16
IT'S OK 18
TRUST YOURSELF 20
WORDS TO KNOW 22
FOR MORE INFORMATION 23
INDEX 24

BOLDFACE WORDS APPEAR IN WORDS TO KNOW.

LISTEN IN

Feelings are your body's way of talking to you. Learning how to listen to your feelings is an important part of growing up! Sometimes feelings can be **overwhelming**. Don't be scared. Instead, get **curious**! Ask yourself, what are my feelings telling me?

LISTENING TO YOUR FEELINGS IS A GREAT WAY TO GET TO KNOW YOURSELF!

NAME THAT FEELING

When you're overcome with feelings, it helps to name them. Here's a list of some big feelings:
- happy
- mad
- excited
- sad
- scared
- **frustrated**

Sometimes you feel a few different feelings all at once! That's natural too. Never fear your feelings.

HOW ARE YOU FEELING?

7

THE "UH-OH" FEELING

Manny had a bad feeling. His stomach hurt. His heart was pounding. His knees felt shaky. His throat felt tight. It made it hard to breathe. There was a ringing sound in his ears. Manny couldn't think clearly.

FEELINGS ARE FRIENDS

The "uh-oh" feeling can be very powerful. That's because it has an important job. It's your body's way of telling you that you aren't safe! Pay attention to when you get that "uh-oh" feeling. What people are around you? What's happening?

LISTEN TO YOUR FEELINGS. THEY'RE YOUR FRIENDS!

SHARE YOUR FEELINGS

When Gloria feels **uncomfortable** or troubled, she knows what to do. She talks to her dad. Even if her dad can't fix the problem, just sharing her feelings out loud with somebody who loves her helps Gloria feel better.

GLORIA'S DAD MAKES HER FEEL SAFE. WHO MAKES YOU FEEL SAFE?

MAKE A SAFETY CIRCLE

Whether you're worried, scared, or sad, it helps to talk to a safe grown-up. A safety circle is a group of adults you can trust. The people in your safety circle will always listen to you, believe you, and help you. You can tell them anything.

FEELING CONFUSED

Sometimes you may feel **confused**. Your friends might like someone that gives you the "uh-oh" feeling. Why don't you feel comfortable too? When your feelings are confusing, it's time to talk to an adult from your safety circle.

SOMETIMES FEELINGS ARE CONFUSING.

It's OK

Feelings aren't right or wrong. You don't have to feel guilty, or bad, about how you feel. Don't **ignore** your feelings either. If someone gives you an "uh-oh" feeling, share your feelings with a safe adult. You won't get in trouble.

ALL FEELINGS ARE OK.

TRUST YOURSELF

You don't need to ignore hard feelings or talk yourself out of them. Instead, ask questions! When do you feel safe or unsafe? What people are around you? What are you doing? Share your feelings with an adult you trust.

Words to Know

confused: Feeling mixed up or unsure about things.

curious: Wanting to know or learn about something.

frustrated: Feeling angry or bothered.

ignore: To pretend something isn't happening.

overwhelming: Overpowering or hard to deal with.

uncomfortable: Feeling unhappy or unsure.

FOR MORE INFORMATION

BOOKS

McAneney, Caitie. *I Talk to Cope*. New York, NY: PowerKids Press, 2023.

Ridley, Sarah. *Being Safe*. New York, NY: PowerKids Press, 2023.

WEBSITES

Kids Health
kidshealth.org/en/kids/talk-feelings.html
Learn how to talk about your feelings.

PBS Kids
pbskids.org/video/pbs-kids-talk-about/3043600136
Watch this helpful video of real families talking about their feelings.

Publisher's note to educators and parents: Our editors have carefully reviewed these websites to ensure that they are suitable for students. Many websites change frequently, however, and we cannot guarantee that a site's future contents will continue to meet our high standards of quality and educational value. Be advised that students should be closely supervised whenever they access the internet.

INDEX

confused, 16, 17
curious, 4, 20
excited, 6
feeling guilty, 18
frustrated, 6
happy, 6
listening to your feelings, 4, 5, 10, 11, 21
mad, 6
overwhelming, 4

sad, 6, 14
safety circle, 14, 15, 18, 20
scared, 5, 6, 14
sharing your feelings, 12, 20
trust, 20
"uh-oh" feeling, 8, 9, 10, 16, 18
uncomfortable, 12
unsafe, 10, 20
worried, 14